THE BANDIT QUEEN

Natalia and Lauren O'Hara

PUFFIN

To the family we found.

PUFFIN BOOKS

UK | USA | Canada | Ireland | Australia
India | New Zealand | South Africa

Puffin Books is part of the Penguin Random House group of companies
whose addresses can be found at global.penguinrandomhouse.com.

www.penguin.co.uk   www.puffin.co.uk   www.ladybird.co.uk

Penguin
Random House
UK

First published 2018
This edition published 2019

001

Printed in China
A CIP catalogue record for this book is available from the British Library

ISBN: 978-0-141-37903-5

All correspondence to: Puffin Books, Penguin Random House Children's
80 Strand, London WC2R 0RL

The woods are full of horrible sounds
to make you quiver and quake.

The wail of a wolf, a lonely owl's yowl,
the hissssssss of a slithery snake!

But worse than the wail, or the yowl,
or the hiss,
the horridest sound in the woods
sounds like this. . .

"We screech and we roar,
Spit peas on the floor,
We're up banging pots until three.
Though we don't mean to brag –
We're *horribly* bad!
The best of all bandits are we!

"We yell till we're red,
Then bellow instead,
We kick and we throw cutlery.
At being grown men we'd score one out of ten –
    The best of all bandits are we!

"We yodel and crow,
Yell 'Shut it!' and 'NOOOO!'
We are not precise when we pee!
Whatever you do we're *far* worse than you –
    The best of all bandits are we!"

Oh, those bandits were wicked!

Grabby and sneaky . . .

Jealous and cruel.

But the ghastliest thing that they ever did . . .

. . . was rob an orphan school.

They took books and boots and newts,
socks and clocks, a picnic box,
boxer shorts, coloured chalks
and a box of forks.

Back at home
they bent the books,
socked the clocks
and tore the socks,
ate the chalk and . . .
"YeeeeeeUCK!" they spat.
"That is not FOOD!
What's in the box?"

"What *is* that thing?"

"A frilly pig?"

"A no-hair cat?"

"It's small . . .
and *pretty*!"

"TAKE! IT! BACK!"

But when they tried to pick her up, the baby . . .

screeched and roared, and peed on the floor.

Yelled and turned red, then bit them instead.

Yodelled and crowed and hollered "NOOOO!"

"She is *horrible*!" they cried.

"The worst we've ever seen!"

And so . . .

. . . they made her Queen.

"O Bandit Queen!" the bandits crowed.
"Little horror! Poison weed!"

"We will give you *everything* a queen could ever need!"

They gave her baths,

and sing-songs,

tasty things to eat,

lovely clothes,

lots of pets,

education,

and on her birthday
a special treat!

But day by day the Queen grew sad.

"What is it, bugaboo?" they crowed.
"Do you need a shark to ride?
A digger truck? A gemmy treasure trove?"

The Queen whispered, "Why are you such babies?"
A tear dripped off her nose.

"BABIES?" they roared. "Oh, no, no, NO!
We're so *very* grown – you'll see!"

That night they went to the ballet.
They were just as grown
as they could be.

But next morning when
the first light shone . . .

the Queen was gone.

The bandits cried, "She *is*
here really! She's hiding,
just to make us laugh."

"Bandit Queen,
come *home!*"
they crooned.
"We'll give you swords
and stripy scarves."

They roared:
  "What did you *do*?"
  "It was *him!*"
    "*Meeeeee*? It was YOU!"
They kicked and hit
    and bit (or tried).

They lay down on the floor and cried.

Then a small voice whispered,
    "Bandits, hush! What if it was all of us?"

                    Meanwhile . . .

Back at school the Queen learned three times nine . . .

and brushed her teeth . . .

and went to bed . . .

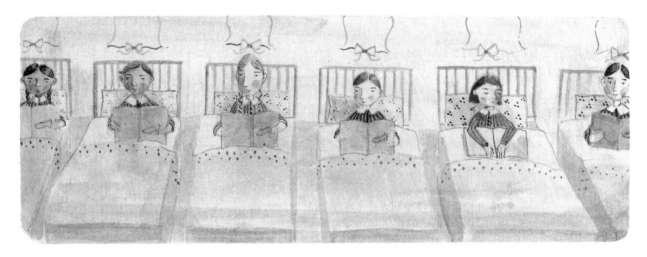

all in a line.

Then from the outside she heard a crow.

It sounded like home! She ran to see. And there, down below . . .

"We yell and we roar,
'Oh, *won't* you have more?
We made this soup especially!'
We'll struggle and fight
To try and do right
And be what you
      need us to be!

"We only pinch cheeks,
Not birds or antiques.
We say, 'Who wants milk in their tea?'
We're learning to write,
To sleep when it's night
        And *never* to bite company!

"We know you felt mad,
And lonely and sad –
We're sorry as sorry can be.
But whatever you do
We'll *always* love you.
        We'll help you be all you can be."

Up in her window,
they heard the Queen gasp . . .
and laugh . . . and say . . .

"It feels scary to grow,
but less when you know
that someone you love
can show you the way!"

Down she hopped.

And the bandits caught her snug,
in a snugly, cuddly bandit hug.

Then they romped and they
rollicked and gambolled and sprung
back home to the woods to find some new fun.

And as the sun rose,
and the bandits all ran,
the little girl smiled . . .

She had a plan.